Jesse and the Seven Wonders of St. John's

Story by:

Herbert F Hopkins

Illustrated by:

Corey Majeau

Copyright

Words and Wood Publishing
22 Flavin Street, Suite 303
ST. John's, NL, A1C3R9
Canada
Canadian Cataloguing in Publication Data
Herbert F Hopkins

Print ISBN: 978-1-7779-150-0-1

Foreword

Imagine how exciting it would be to have a flying pillow that would transport you on adventures at night? Thanks to Jesse and Pilot, you don't have to imagine but can join along in this book by Herbert Hopkins, beautifully illustrated by Corey Majeau. From the top of Signal Hill to the bottom of Deadman's Pond, this book offers a bird's eye view of what makes this a great city – including the importance of making new friends with the new people we meet.

The City of St. John's has many wonderful locations to discover for people of all ages, and I am pleased to see our historic and colourful city featured in this book for children. I will certainly add it to my list to share when I visit schools to read to classes and I'm happy that you, too, are interested in the "seven wonders of St. John's."

Mayor Danny Breen
City of St. John's

Dedication:
to friends

Acknowledgments

Many people have helped to create this book. The first was my neighbour, Bert Riggs, who floated the idea. With a master's hand, Susan Flanagan edited the work. My hawk-eyed test readers, Sheilagh O'Leary and Jane Dennison added the finishing touches. From the beginning, illustrator, Corey Majeau embraced my story, and throughout the process, filled it with colour, imagination and joy.

A special thank you to His Worship, Mayor Danny Breen for writing the forward and to Andy Jones for his kind words.

A heap of thanks to my wife, Jane, who is always there for help and support, and of course to the one and only Pirate, aka Pilot, our handsome one-eyed mutt.

Lastly, thank you to the city of St John's, my home and inspiration. What a spot!

Author's note

Thank you for picking up a copy of "Jesse and the Seven Wonders of St. John's." I hope you enjoy my little story.

You may wonder why "seven" was chosen as the number of wonders; why not ten or twenty, or in the case of St. John's, even hundreds. In ancient Greece where the original wonders of the world were chosen, the number seven was thought to represent perfection. So seven it was then and seven it is today.

Hey Kids!

If you look carefully at the illustrations, you will find objects in groups of seven. How many can you find? Check out the Jesse website to see if your answers are correct. Maybe win a prize.

www.jesseandthesevenwonders.com

While you're at it, have a listen to the author's song, "Jesse's Dream;" sung and played by Bob MacDonald and accompanied by Gerry Strong. Enjoy!

www.jesseandthesevenwonders.com/audio/song.mp3

This week's assignment

The Seven Wonders of St John's

Roan!

Mrs. House

Science Fair Sign- Ups

Monday morning at School with Mrs. House

"Good morning, class, today we look at home,
the place we love to be,
our city on a rugged rock,
on the edge of the open sea.

"From John Cabot to this day,
it's the sea that this place knows,
and the wind, the tireless wind,
that keeps us on our toes.

"Much has changed since the mighty cod,
did fill the fishers' hold,
but, still the wonder of this place
is something to behold.

"So, class, your work this week,
is through your town to roam,
to see the seven wonders,
that make St. John's your home."

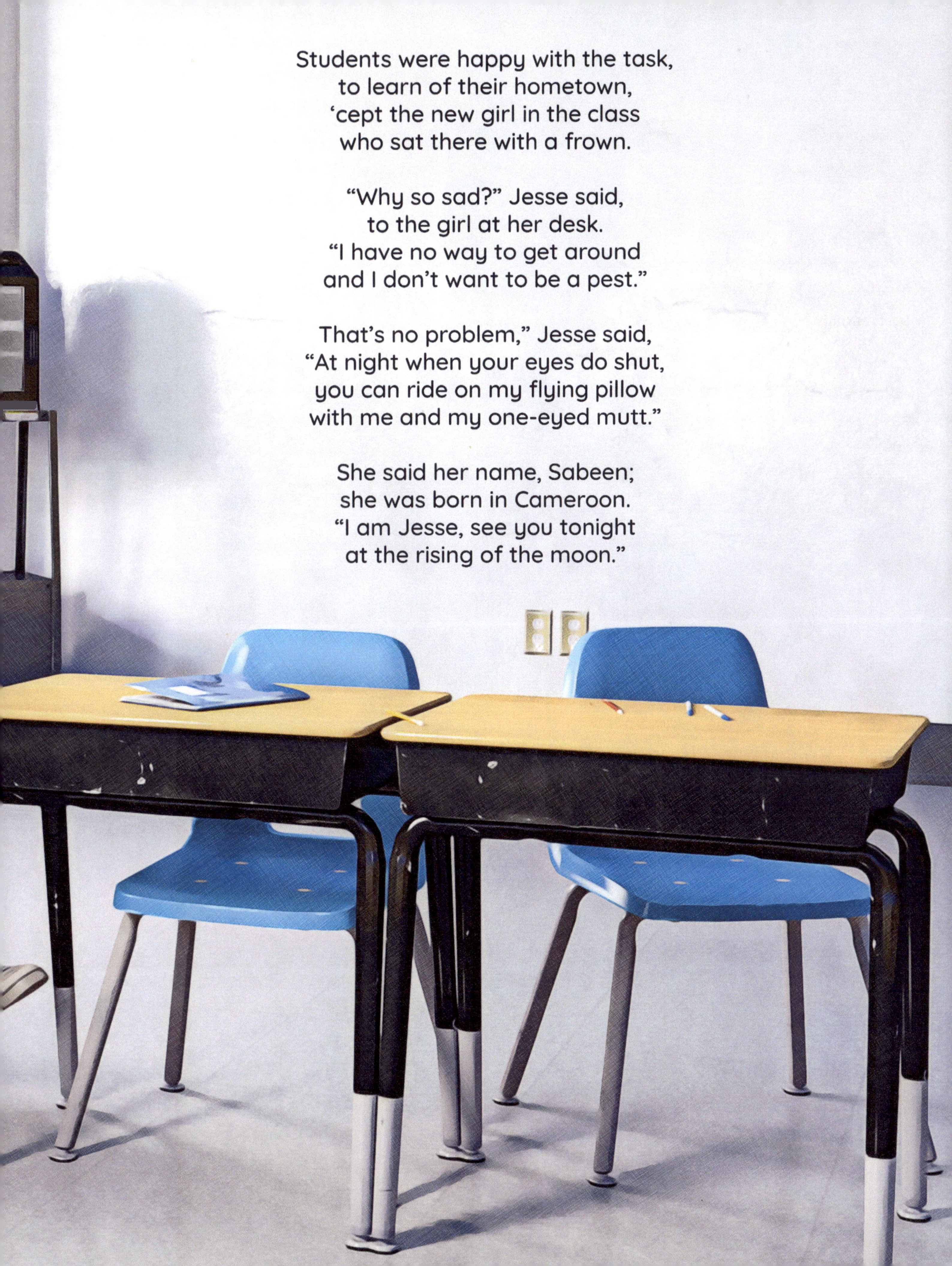

Students were happy with the task,
to learn of their hometown,
'cept the new girl in the class
who sat there with a frown.

"Why so sad?" Jesse said,
to the girl at her desk.
"I have no way to get around
and I don't want to be a pest."

That's no problem," Jesse said,
"At night when your eyes do shut,
you can ride on my flying pillow
with me and my one-eyed mutt."

She said her name, Sabeen;
she was born in Cameroon.
"I am Jesse, see you tonight
at the rising of the moon."

Later that night in Jesse's Dreams

"It's time to go, my one-eyed mutt
to some places I've never seen,
but first let's make some room
for my new friend, named Sabeen."

Pilot grabbed a second pillow
and tied it on real tight,
then in our dreams, off we flew
into the St. John's night.

And there was Sabeen, with a gracious smile,
bigger than the moon,
"Hop on board," I said to her,
"You can see there's lots of room."

"To **SIGNAL HILL**, my one-eyed navigator,
a wonderous place to be!
The Atlantic Ocean and the city lights
as far as you can see!"

Behold the tower to honour Cabot,
and the flags for signalling ships to port,
and the spot where Marconi made his mark
with signals of a different sort.

And the lighthouses across the Narrows
from Fort Amherst to Cape Spear
and trails and whales, and icebergs
and the call of the cannoneer.

And the stages at the water's edge,
where folks once worked the sea.
With their gardens of granite walls
at home in the Battery.

"This is the best," said Sabeen.
"I'm so happy to be free."
"But in our dreams tomorrow night," I said,
"There are more sights to see."

"To **THE ROOMS**, my one-eyed navigator."
A treasure trove of stories,
of masterpieces and artifacts,
soldiers and wooden dories.

Like the old-time fisher shed
of yarns, bait, and gear
these giant rooms of stone and steel
hold the treasures we revere.

Then outside the swinging door
under sun or rain,
the spirit of art was everywhere
on every city lane.

Said Sabeen, "My mother played the harp,
before she was lost at sea.
Of the few things she left behind,
her songs are most dear to me."

"So sorry for your loss," I said.
"But glad you have the songs.
And tomorrow, there'll be another dream,
we hope you'll come along."

"To **QUIDI VIDI**, my one-eyed navigator.
and the Regatta on the lake.
But the wind is high, it may be cancelled,
So the scenic route we'll take."

"Is that the lake down there?"
Sabeen asked from her pillow perch.
then she stood, and the wind did gust,
and the pillow began to lurch.

She stumbled, and lost her balance;
into Deadman's Pond, she fell.
"Oh my, that pond is bottomless,
or so the legends tell."

Pilot leapt from the pillow
into the darkened still
"I see her sinking," Jesse called,
from a spot on Gibbet Hill.

Pilot dove into the deep
for what seemed to be forever,
until my one-eyed dog spotted Sabeen,
and attached her to a tether.

Pilot paddled to the surface
with Sabeen safely in tow
to see again the stars above
with her face all aglow.

"Oh Jesse, I saw my mother's face,
I was deep as deep can be,
she smiled and said she loved me
and that her soul can now be free."

"Let's get you home," I said.
"To get you warm and dry.
But on our pillow tomorrow
we'll give it another try."

"To QUIDI VIDI, again, my one-eyed navigator,
where the wind has made its call,
for the rowers to set their shells
on the pond to give their all.

And after the pondside games
if you need a little rest,
then the little cove in the village,
should be your quiet quest.

Quidi Vidi or Quida Vida,
It doesn't matter what,
for all the people living here
they simply say, The Gut.

Then there are the buried tunnels
locked beneath the ground
with legends of a pirate's treasure
never yet been found.

"I want to live here," said Sabeen.
"Such a joyous place to be"
"in our dreams tomorrow night," I said.
"There's another place to see."

"To **ST. JOHN'S HARBOUR,** my one-eyed navigator."
Explorers, captains, and crew,
Draggers, dories, and drill ships,
supply vessels, cruise ships too.

Once the ships did fill the harbour,
you could leap from deck to deck,
from the south side to the harbour front,
without ever getting wet.

And the Narrows, the city's guard,
a passageway from the sea
to thread the needle into the harbour
for cargo, or storms to flee.

And then, there are the harbour legends
and my favourite one I'll share,
a mermaid sprawled across Chain Rock
brushing her long blond hair.

"This is the best," said Sabeen.
"What a wonderous place to be."

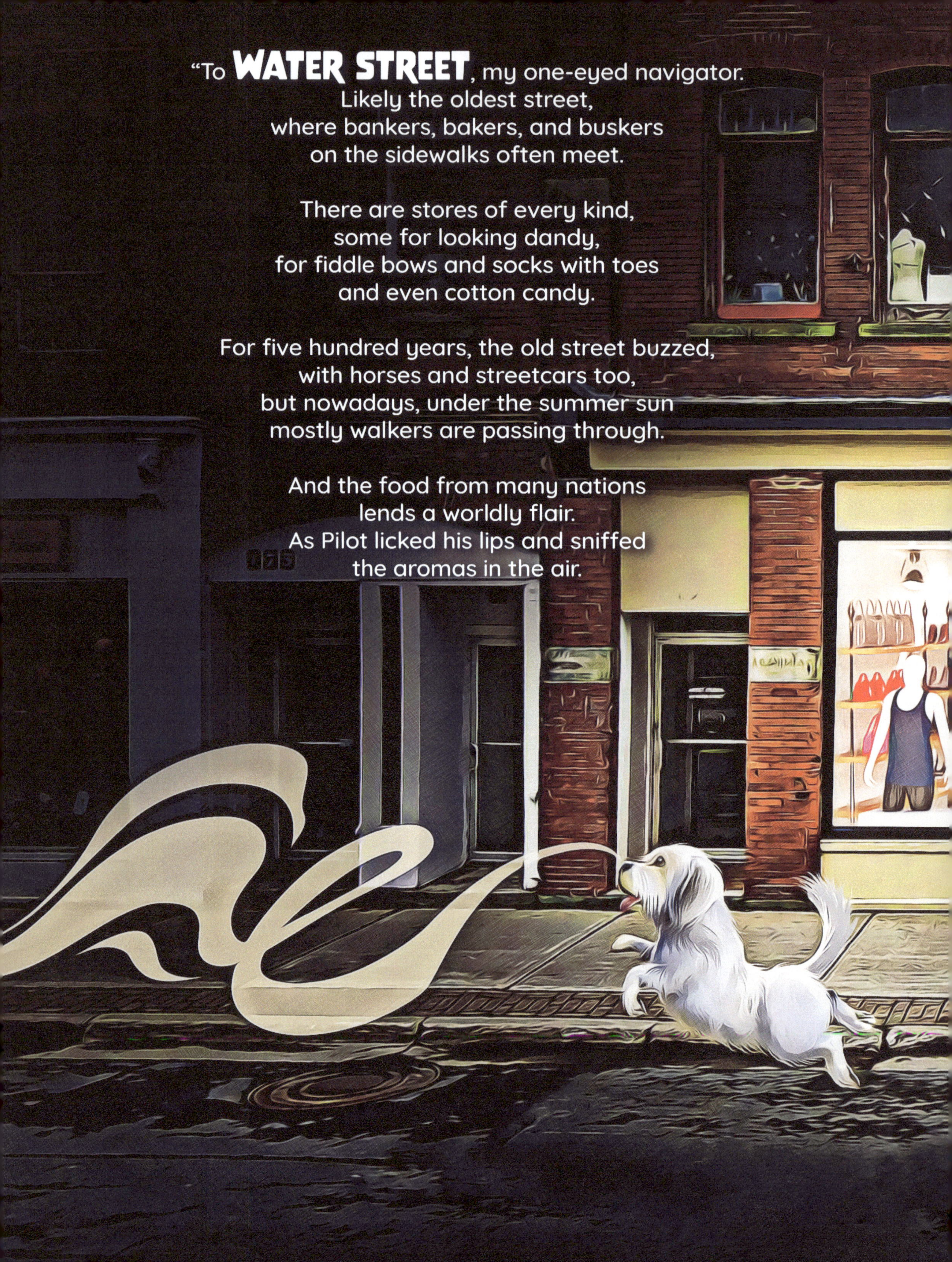

"To **WATER STREET**, my one-eyed navigator.
Likely the oldest street,
where bankers, bakers, and buskers
on the sidewalks often meet.

There are stores of every kind,
some for looking dandy,
for fiddle bows and socks with toes
and even cotton candy.

For five hundred years, the old street buzzed,
with horses and streetcars too,
but nowadays, under the summer sun
mostly walkers are passing through.

And the food from many nations
lends a worldly flair.
As Pilot licked his lips and sniffed
the aromas in the air.

7
NEWFOUNDLAND WEAVERY
177
"This is the best," said Sabeen.
"What a wonderous place to be."
"And tomorrow there'll be another dream," I said.
"There are more sights to see."

"I love it here," said Sabeen.
"Being with you and Pilot too."
"It was great fun" I said.
"And tomorrow our work is due."

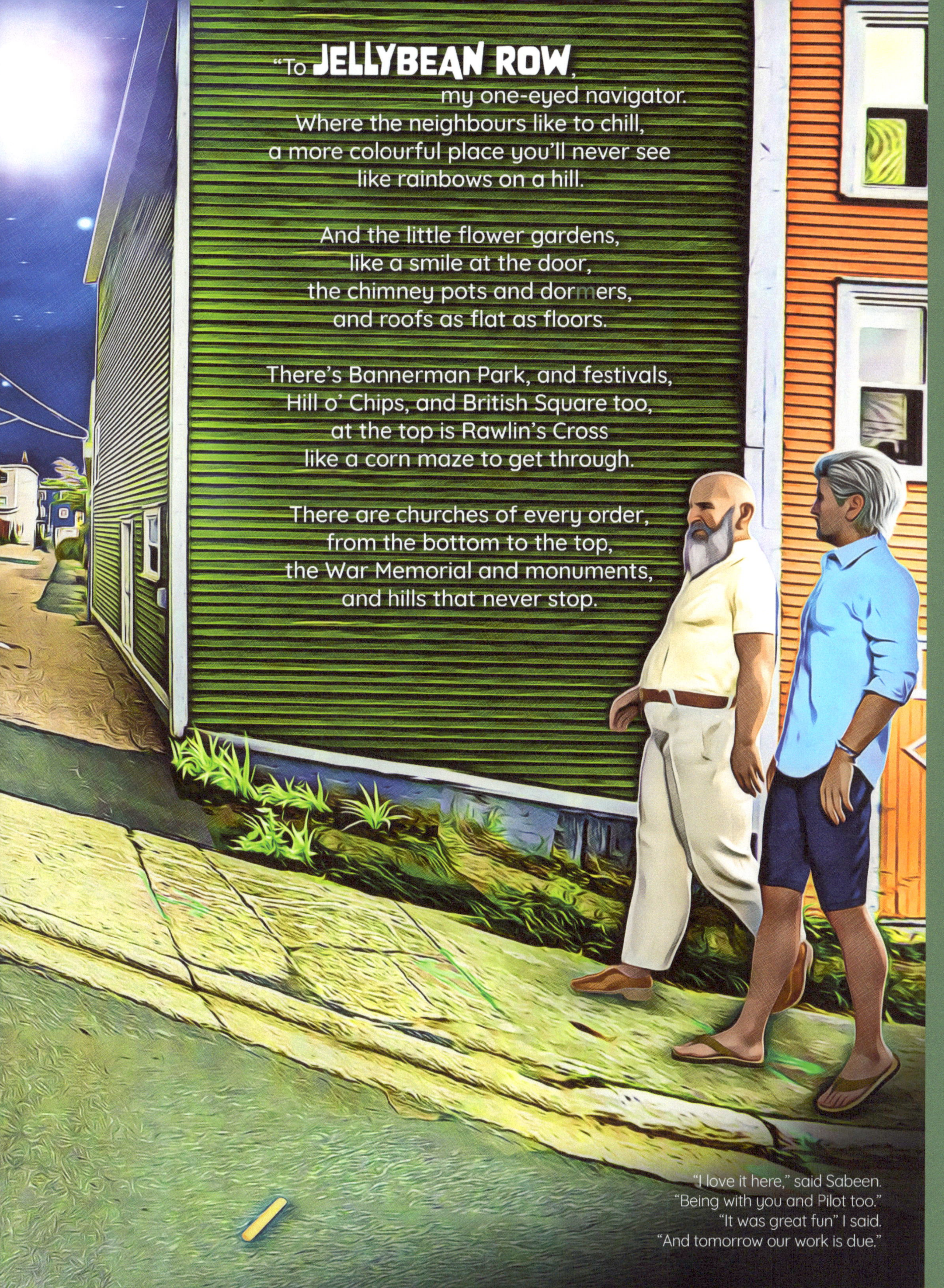
"To JELLYBEAN ROW,
my one-eyed navigator.
Where the neighbours like to chill,
a more colourful place you'll never see
like rainbows on a hill.

And the little flower gardens,
like a smile at the door,
the chimney pots and dormers,
and roofs as flat as floors.

There's Bannerman Park, and festivals,
Hill o' Chips, and British Square too,
at the top is Rawlin's Cross
like a corn maze to get through.

There are churches of every order,
from the bottom to the top,
the War Memorial and monuments,
and hills that never stop.

"I love it here," said Sabeen.
"Being with you and Pilot too."
"It was great fun" I said.
"And tomorrow our work is due."

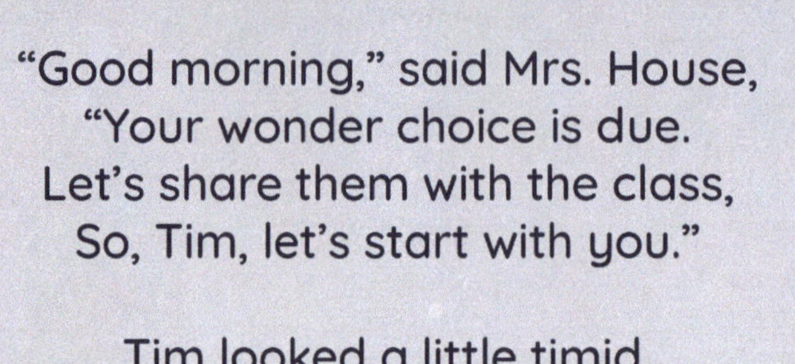

"Good morning," said Mrs. House,
"Your wonder choice is due.
Let's share them with the class,
So, Tim, let's start with you."

Tim looked a little timid.
"Wish I had my work to show,
But a gust of wind did grab it,
And out the Narrows it did blow."

"Oh my," said Mrs. House,
"Jill, what would you like to say?"
"My favourite is the War Memorial,
to give thanks for peace today."

"That's very good, Jill. And Jesse,
I know you have the means,
to travel near and far,
on a pillow in your dreams."

"Oh yes, Miss, I saw the wonders,
and all were quite a thrill,
the Harbour, the Rooms, Jellybean Row,
Quidi Vidi, Water Street and the Hill."

"But that's only six,"
Mrs. House did say.
"And your favourite wonder;
do you have it here today?"

At that moment, all went quiet
No desk did make a squeak
Then, Sabeen who seldom spoke
Raised her hand to speak.

"As you know, I'm new to here,
and everything was wrong,
I was sad and had no friends,
until Jesse came along.

And with Jesse and Pilot, I learned so much,
about the wonders great and small,

BUT IT'S YOUR FRIENDS THAT ARE THE GREATEST WONDER,

for they help you when you fall."

MRS. HOUSE'S CLASS
7 Wonders Of St. John's
1. The Harbour
2. The Rooms
3. Jellybean Row
4. Quidi Vidi
5. Water Street
6. The Hill
7.

"Bravo," said Mrs. House,
"What a perfect observation,
and thank you Sabeen, Jesse, and Pilot,
you are all an inspiration."

WOOF   **THE END**

Jesse's Dream

by Herbert F Hopkins

2
12
G
Dmaj7
F#m/C#
3
wel-come than the spring- time
filled with love and care
Re-mem-ber the grea-test
15
G
A7
A7
won-der
as you will sure-ly learn
it's a place that when youleave it
you al-ways
will re
19
Dmaj7
D7
G
tum
23
Dmaj7
Dmaj7
la la la la la la
la la la la la
25
D7
rit.
G
Dmaj7
la la la la la la la
la la la la la

Herbert F Hopkins

Herbert F Hopkins has written and published three novels. He has also written a book of poetry which was acquired by the National Library of Canada for its National Book Preservation Centre.

More recently, Hopkins has turned has hand to writing children's books, firstly penning the internationally recognized "Jesse and the Seven Wonders of the World," and now "Jesse and the Seven Wonders of St. John's." Hopkins has been fortunate to have collaborated with some of Newfoundland's finest artists like Boyd Chubbs, Marin Darmonkow and Corey Majeau.

Hopkins lives in St. John's with his beautiful wife, Jane, and their one-eyed mutt, Pirate (aka Pilot).

Visit him at www.wordsandwood.ca and www.jesseandthesevenwonders.com.

Corey Majeau

Corey Majeau is an author, illustrator, and cartoonist born in Edson, Alberta. After falling in love with the rocky shores of Newfoundland, he decided to make it his home. Corey has been a cartoonist and graphic designer for over a decade, with his work spread across multiple platforms and small presses. His cover designs have been nominated for several awards and featured in numerous bestselling titles. He resides in Gander, NL, with his wofe and best friend, Candace, their son Jack, and daughter Charlie.